Dear Parents and Educators,

Welcome to Penguin Young Readers! As parents and educators, you know that each child develops at his or her own pace—in terms of speech, critical thinking, and, of course, reading. Penguin Young Readers recognizes this fact. As a result, each Penguin Young Readers book is assigned a traditional easy-to-read level (1–4) as well as a Guided Reading Level (A–P). Both of these systems will help you choose the right book for your child. Please refer to the back of each book for specific leveling information. Penguin Young Readers features esteemed authors and illustrators, stories about favorite characters, fascinating nonfiction, and more!

Busy Bugs
A Book About Patterns

LEVEL 2

GUIDED READING LEVEL **F**

This book is perfect for a **Progressing Reader** who:
• can figure out unknown words by using picture and context clues;
• can recognize beginning, middle, and ending sounds;
• can make and confirm predictions about what will happen in the text; and
• can distinguish between fiction and nonfiction.

Here are some **activities** you can do during and after reading this book:
• Make Connections: The bugs love making patterns! For example, they place flowers two by two—two red flowers, then two blue flowers. They use different colors and even different bugs to make patterns. On a separate sheet of paper, draw pictures to create patterns of your own.
• Rhyming Words: Find the rhyming words in the story. On a separate sheet of paper, write each word next to the word it rhymes with. Use the chart below as an example.

Word	Rhymes with
fast	last
go	show
spots	dots

Remember, sharing the love of reading with a child is the best gift you can give!

—Bonnie Bader, EdM
  Penguin Young Readers program

*Penguin Young Readers are leveled by independent reviewers applying the standards developed by Irene Fountas and Gay Su Pinnell in *Matching Books to Readers: Using Leveled Books in Guided Reading*, Heinemann, 1999.

To my American grandmothers,
Marnie and Laura, who always save room
for my books on their coffee table—BA

Penguin Young Readers
Published by the Penguin Group
Penguin Group (USA) Inc., 375 Hudson Street, New York, New York 10014, USA
Penguin Group (Canada), 90 Eglinton Avenue East, Suite 700, Toronto, Ontario M4P 2Y3, Canada
(a division of Pearson Penguin Canada Inc.)
Penguin Books Ltd., 80 Strand, London WC2R 0RL, England
Penguin Group Ireland, 25 St. Stephen's Green, Dublin 2, Ireland (a division of Penguin Books Ltd.)
Penguin Group (Australia), 250 Camberwell Road, Camberwell, Victoria 3124, Australia
(a division of Pearson Australia Group Pty. Ltd.)
Penguin Books India Pvt. Ltd., 11 Community Centre, Panchsheel Park, New Delhi—110 017, India
Penguin Group (NZ), 67 Apollo Drive, Rosedale, Auckland 0632, New Zealand
(a division of Pearson New Zealand Ltd.)
Penguin Books (South Africa) (Pty.) Ltd., 24 Sturdee Avenue,
Rosebank, Johannesburg 2196, South Africa

Penguin Books Ltd., Registered Offices: 80 Strand, London WC2R 0RL, England

Library of Congress Control Number: 2003004837

ISBN 978-0-448-43159-8   10 9 8 7 6 5 4 3 2 1

BUSY BUGS

A Book About Patterns

by Jayne Harvey
illustrated by Bernard Adnet

Penguin Young Readers
An Imprint of Penguin Group (USA) Inc.

The busy bugs are moving fast.

A special day has come at last.

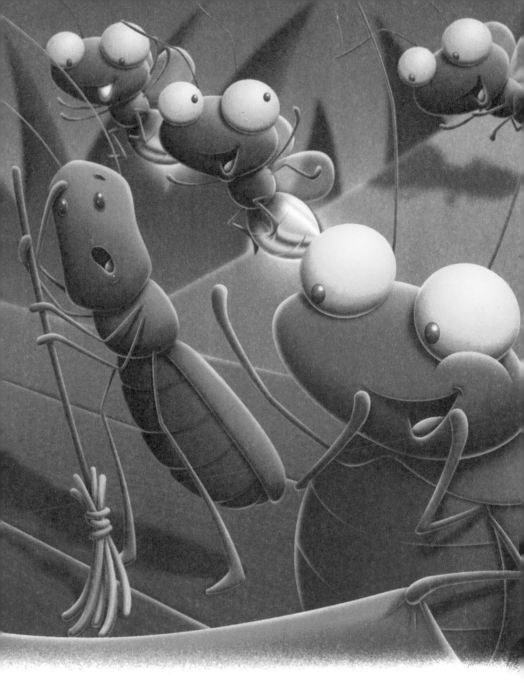

They make patterns as they go,

getting ready for the show.

The ladybugs

must shine their spots.

Each red wing

has three black dots.

Butterflies clean

their matching wings.

"Oh, how pretty!"

a cricket sings.

The spiders go

around and around.

They spin their webs

down to the ground.

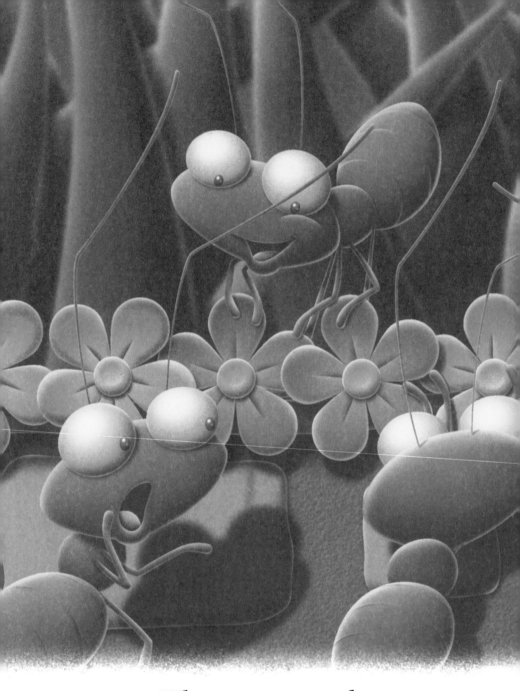

The ants spend

many busy hours

making patterns

with the flowers.

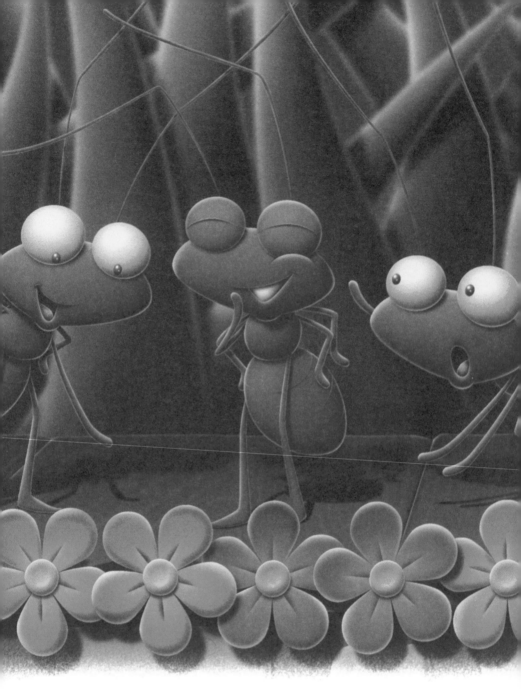

They place the flowers

two by two.

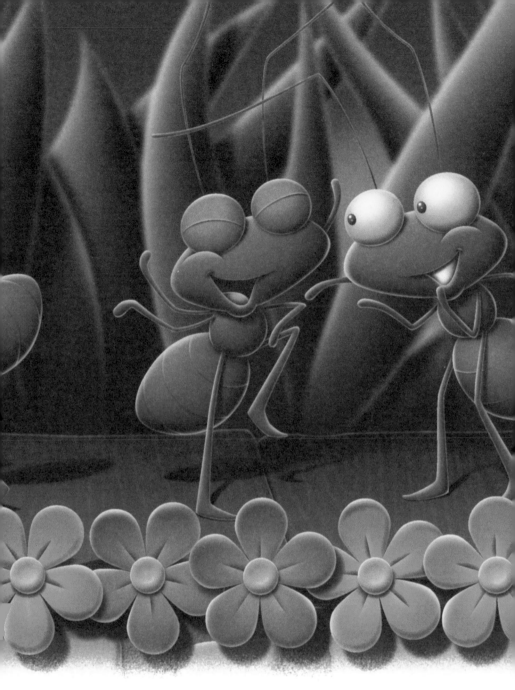

First red, then blue.

Then red, then blue.

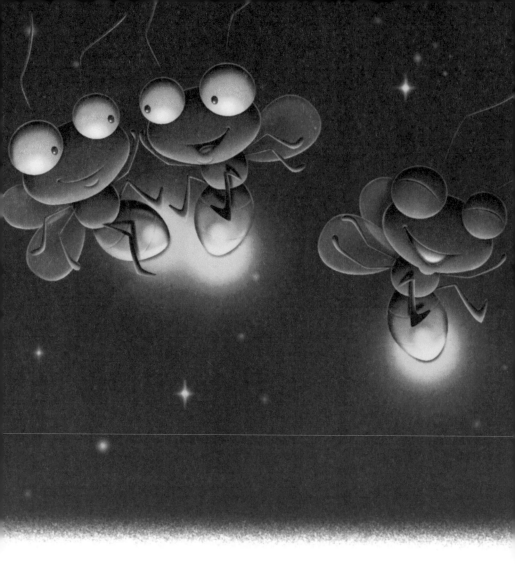

The fireflies will make

things bright.

Each firefly shines

with yellow light.

They make a pattern

just for fun.

Two lights, then one.

Two lights, then one.

Now the bugs are ready to go.

It is time to start the show.

Here are eight bugs

who like to sing.

They all line up

from wing to wing.

One moth, one flea,

one fly, one bee.

One moth, one flea,

one fly, one bee.

Look over there!

Here come the ants.

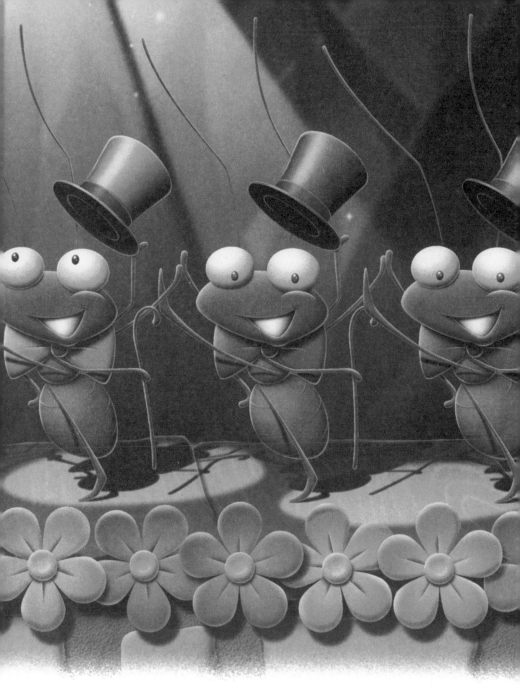

They want to show off

their new dance.

They make a pattern

as they glide.

Hop, hop, slide!

Hop, hop, slide!

Now the fireflies

take flight.

They make bright loops

in the night.

The next act is

the best of all!

The bugs stack up

from big to small.

Six beetles, five spiders,

and four bees.

Three flies, two ants,

and one small flea.

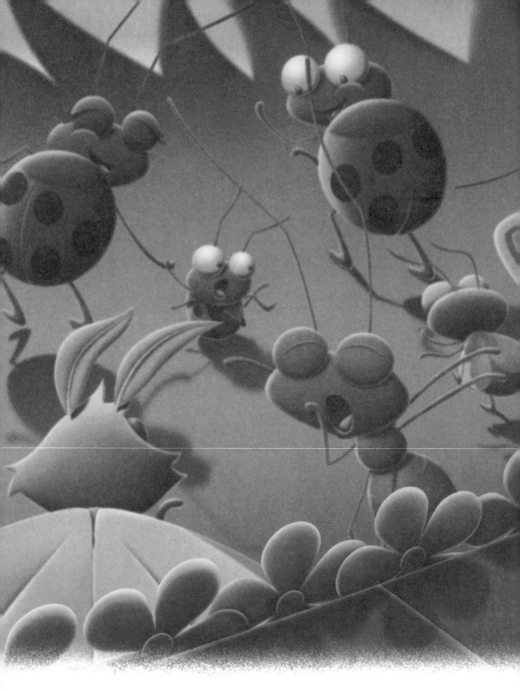

The night is done.

Here comes the sun!

The show is over.

The bugs had fun.

Now the busy bugs can rest.

The bug show really was the best!